MW00905387

To Anne McNeil

Other Baby Bear books to share:

The Big Baby Bear Book
Again!
Walking Round the Garden
Number One, Tickle Your Tum
The Bear Went Over the Mountain
Oh Where, Oh Where?

First edition for the United States, its dependencies, the Philippines, and
Canada published in 2003 by Barron's Educational Series, Inc.

First published in 2002 in Great Britain by The Bodley Head,
an imprint of Random House Children's Books

All inquiries should be addressed to:
Barron's Educational Series, Inc.
250 Wireless Boulevard
Hauppauge, New York 11788
http://www.barronseduc.com

Library of Congress Catalog Card No.: 2002104345
International Standard Book No.: 0-7641-2304-1

Printed and bound in Singapore
9 8 7 6 5 4 3 2 1

HOLD TIGHT!

JOHN PRATER

BARRON'S

Grandbear was busy . . .

Baby Bear was
busy, too.

"*Vroom, vroom!* I'm on a plane," said Baby Bear. "Want to come?"

"OK. Just a quick ride then," said Grandbear.

"HOLD TIGHT!"

"Hip, hip, hooray,
We're on our way,
Flying high and low . . ."

"But now
we're flying
upside down . . ."

"... and over we all go! Now I must do the laundry."

But before Grandbear could pick up the laundry, Baby Bear scrambled back into the box.

"Now what?" asked Grandbear.
"*Choo-choo! Choo-choo!* I'm on a train,"
said Baby Bear. "Want to come?"
"OK. Just a quick ride then,"
said Grandbear.

"HOLD TIGHT!"

"Hip, hip, hooray,
We're on our way,
Going very
slowly . . ."

"But faster now,
and faster still . . ."

" . . . and over we all go! Now I must do the laundry."

But before Grandbear could pick up the laundry basket, Baby Bear scrambled into it.

"Now what?"
asked
Grandbear.

"*Splish, splash!* I'm on a boat,"
said Baby Bear. "Want to come?"
Grandbear sighed and said, "OK,
just a very quick ride, but then I
must get going."

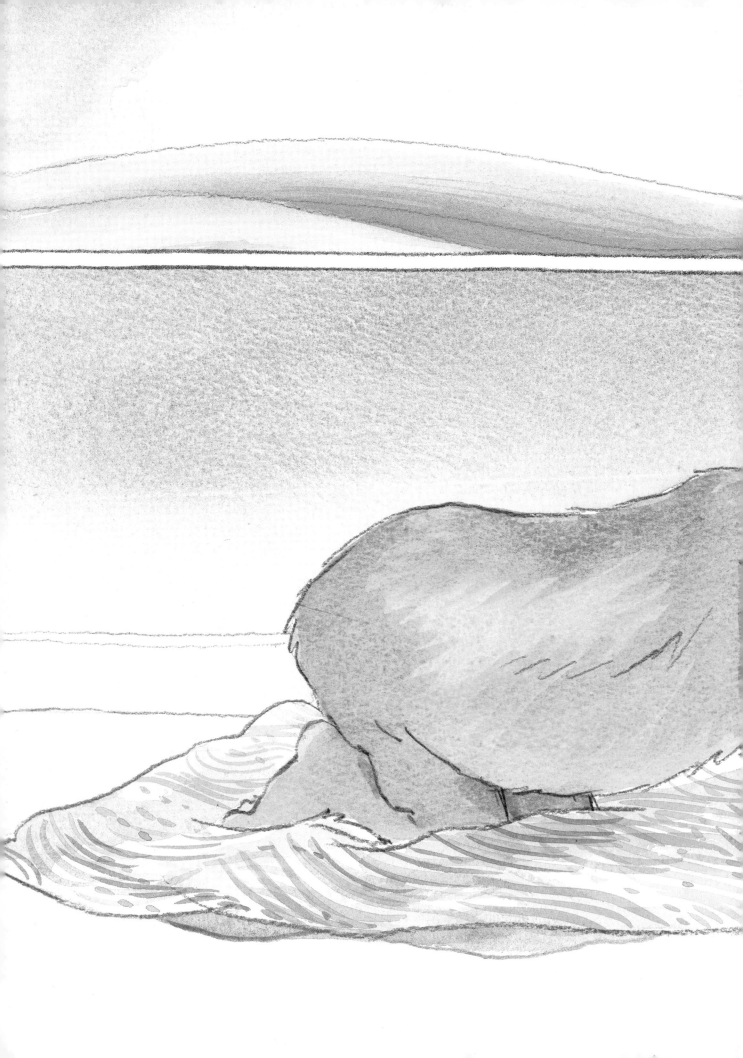

"HOLD TIGHT!"

"Hip, hip, hooray,
We're on our way,
Bobbing to and fro.
But, look!
Here comes a
great big wave . . ."

" . . . and over we all go!"

"Now I really *must* do the laundry," said Grandbear.

"OK," said Baby Bear. "Can I come?"

"HOLD TIGHT!"

"Hip, hip, hooray,
We're on our way
To get the laundry done.
We've ridden on a plane,
A boat,
A train,
We've had a lot of fun . . ."

"... and HERE WE ARE!"

"Oh," said Baby Bear.
"Just one more ride.
Pleeease!"

"All right," said Grandbear.
"Just *one* more. And this
will be the very best ride of all."

"HOLD TIGHT!"